*Title: **The Deadly Love***
*Subtitle: **Vampire MF Romance Story***
*Author: **Leona Harris***

© **Copyright 2022 by Leona Harris. All rights reserved.**

No part of this publication may be reproduced, distributed, or transmitted in any form or by any means, including photocopying, recording, or other electronic or mechanical methods, or by any information storage and retrieval system without the prior written permission of the publisher, except in the case of very brief quotations embodied in critical reviews and certain other noncommercial uses permitted by copyright law.

This is a work of fiction. Any resemblance to any person, living or dead is purely coincidental.

From the Publisher:
Thank you for purchasing this book.

Table of Contents

The Deadly Love
Description

Maria made a deal with a vampire who posed as a young man called Leonardo. She was supposed to give up her daughter when she got to the age of thirty-five to become his wife. Along the way, she changed her mind and allowed her daughter, Rosetta, to date whoever she wanted.

Strangely, all the men who declared interest in her ended up mysteriously dying. Maria and her husband, Antonio, eventually got tired and decided to help their daughter in the search of a husband. It didn't take long since their family friend and business partner, Lorenzo, had a son who had married a non-Mexican and was planning to divorce her.

A chance presented itself before them. Lorenzo's son, Eduardo, was asked to marry Rosetta and maintain the family business. But all those plans came crumbling down as Leonardo came back for Rosetta just as agreed. She was his and no one could take her away from him!

Chapter 1

"Will you marry me Rosetta and make me the happiest man in the world?" he posed the long-awaited question.

It was a moment of silence as people waited anxiously to witness the couple make their vows. Everyone moved closer, with profound feelings of disquiet. It all came to a standstill as hope engulfed through Eduardo's feet. He was so excited to hear her say yes!

Unlike Eduardo, Rosetta was swimming in a river of doubt. There was fear that erupted from deep within her that made her lose her focus. She had desired such a moment for a long time but not with Eduardo. She felt like she was just a victim of circumstances, and there was no way she could change that.

She remained silent and seemed carried away for a moment. Her eyes were glued to the clouds as if looking for answers to something totally unrelated to Eduardo. Everything around her suddenly changed. The guests were filled with confusion as they stared at each other with funny guesses and weird glances.

The party then turned gloomy and so did the groom. The bride to be feigned a smile as the weather disapproved of her actions. Loud claps of thunder filled the space as if trying to retaliate for the emotional damage that was about to go down. The sudden changes in the weather made it even harder for the invited guests to blend as they all quickly went back to the hall. It was going to rain soon and the party was also going to end! Probably or possibly!

Eduardo remained on his knees still waiting for her response. He wore his usual broad smile. He had to give her time to answer his question. There was no need to jump to conclusions and assume she didn't want to marry him because according to him, she wanted that! She had told him.

Eduardo had a great smile. It was something that made it easier for him to put coworkers and clients at ease. It helped him make good relations even in the corporate world as he got clients with his personality. And now, even with all the bad signs staring ruthlessly at him, he believed Rosetta was in love with him and would certainly say yes to his marriage proposal. He maintained his cool.

Deep inside, he was filled with gratitude. Eduardo could not believe that it was all coming to pass. Thoughts of how their life would be as a couple crowded his mind. He was ready to grant her biggest wishes. He wanted to give her the exact wedding of her dreams. Make her feel like a queen that she was—just anything and everything for her to be happy. He could not help but picture himself sleeping next to her cuddling with her and waking up to see her beautiful face every morning. She was going to be his sunshine and there was no doubt about that. It was going to be the best experience in his life. Sadly, it was not the same for Rosetta.

Rosetta had a different mindset. Her reasoning did not match the guests. While many saw the engagement as a love bond, she saw it clearly as a business deal. Protection of business interests from both families. A reality that none of her family members wanted to admit.

Rosetta wanted a relationship that would grow from mere attraction to a strong bond. A beautiful feeling that would make her sleepless, stimulated by a touch from someone she loved. She would be so proud talking about their first meeting, how life had been since their first encounter.

Sadly, the man could offer that was Leonardo, and thinking about their last meeting only made her hate herself. She was in love with him, yet she had asked him to keep away since the marriage had already been set by both families. There was no turning back. Leonardo did not leave without giving her something to think about.

"I said you have to go! My engagement party is tomorrow. This can't work! And you need to stop visiting!" She had told him the previous night. He prepared to leave but he had something to say before he did. Rosetta looked out into the darkness as the shadow before her claiming to be Leonardo spoke. She had never seen his face as he always visited at night and never allowed her to see him. According to Rosetta, he was a strange man. Maybe if he were posing like a real human, all the weirdness would come to an end.

"I don't dispute that. Everything is set So what. Is that what you want? Because if it is, I'll stop bothering you. I'll let you be!" Leonardo had questions. He knew that she did not love Eduardo and was only with him because of her father. He also knew that she was madly in love with him. She was just scared. Little did he know that the questions he was asking opened her eyes...

"Maybe, you have a point. The problem is how do I dump a real man...I mean a man who has a face for a faceless man like you! Who are you anyway?" she was tired of his innuendos. If he really wanted them to have a real relationship then he had to show his face!

"I understand. You're scared of saying no to Eduardo and then coming back to your lonely bed?" He was moved by her words. He came closer and held her hands rubbing them smoothly.

"One day I'll visit you. It could be tomorrow. I don't know. But what I know for sure is that I'll show you my face, and I will definitely take you home with me. There will be no engagement, none of all that. I'll take you with me wherever I go. You are the love of my life and I know you love me too....and so you know, it might be sooner than you think." And with that, he left.

Rosetta loved Leonardo no matter who he was. Even though he was behaving weird, she felt she could live with that. There was something so strong about him that made it harder to stay apart. Every night Leonardo visited at wee hours, and would find her waiting for him. She dressed up and looked good for him way before he came. Even though she never saw his real face, it was not the same for him. He claimed that he could see her clearly even in the dark.

Rosetta started looking at Eduardo in a different perspective. She realized that she was making a huge mistake by marrying someone she didn't love just because she wanted to impress her parents. And after Leonardo left, she couldn't sleep. She spent hours turning and crying as she waited for dawn to rise.

The look on her father's face in the morning made all her efforts to pull out of the marriage plans futile. She lost the hope she had the night before when Leonardo visited. Hopelessness took charge and there was no way out of it.

There was something not adding up about her mother. She had started withdrawing away from the planned marriage but she could not show it openly. Two days ago, she had asked her daughter to forgive her. She couldn't go against her husband. It made Rosetta understand that her mother was not for the idea but was playing along.

Mixed emotions made it harder for her. A part of her wanted to say yes and make her daddy proud but her heart was saying no. It constantly reminded her that she had strong feelings for someone else. She wanted to opt out but wait. Her father's wrath would certainly bring her down. She was not supposed to question him. It was disrespectful.

"Will you marry me, sweetheart?" Eduardo repeated his question. Rosetta was shocked and almost jumped out of her shoes. She had forgotten about the engagement. There was something troubling about Eduardo. His tone had suddenly changed and he was almost losing it. He was demanding and was displaying anger toward her. He had noticed the recent change in her but he was not going to face his family in shame again—not after divorcing his wife. It had to work by all means!

All was going on smoothly, until a middle-aged man walked in. She was about to say "yes" but instead she let out a whisper. Nobody heard it as it was not loud enough. She couldn't get her eyes of him. He was smartly dressed in the same clothes as Eduardo.

They were both dressed in black and but the new man had a beard and long hair. He went straight to Rosetta and then smiled at her. He then stretched his hand and shook hers, then took his seat. Nobody understood what was going on. After the young man took his seat, Rosetta followed him, leaving Eduardo on his knees holding a ring.

Something needed to be done since Eduardo was mad. Eduardo stood up angrily and went to get his woman who was already in the new man's arms. He was about to punch him when Maria walked in. She had gone to the washroom and didn't see the new man walk in.

It was Leonardo!

Chapter 2

"Leonardo! Leonardo!" she shouted. Everyone turned to look at her. They thought she was sick but she wasn't. Maria knew exactly what was going on. Leonardo had been forced to come after she refused to honor her end of bargain. It was not business as usual!

"Please I beg you, don't hurt her. She's a good woman Leonardo, please don't hurt her!" She was crying. The guests exchanged glances wondering what was going on.

"I know she is Maria. Don't you worry. She is our princess! How could I forget that?" He was laughing hysterically. Rosetta's father decided to defuse the situation. He came and took his wife away but she continued screaming at the top of her voice as they left.

"He's going to kill all of us! You should let him marry Rosetta!" She left the hall and immediately after, Rosetta could not hide her joy. The kind of warmth she felt in his arms was heavenly. He looked more handsome than she had thought. She needed to be with him. She clung to his hands as he made her feel at peace with herself.

All that time, Eduardo was in rage. He could not believe that Rosetta had walked away from him. She acted like he meant nothing to her, treating him like he didn't matter. It cut him deep. He looked at the wedding ring he had bought for her only to be turned down. He tried to hit Leonardo but he was too strong for him. He held Eduardo's hand and broke it. Leonardo then lifted him up and threw him through the window. He was so wild and was roaring like an animal. When the guests saw that, they started running and within no time, the hall was empty. Not even Eduardo's father remained. He had to run for his life!

***

There was a lot going on in Rosetta's family. Her father wanted her to start a family of her own citing that most of the women her age have married and settled down. She begged him to listen to her but he said they had better plans for her. He was planning to get her a husband in two weeks or so! Little did he know, it was going to result to more pain than healing his daughter's broken heart.

Time moved quickly. Antonio brought the news just as he had promised. Her father informed her that he had arranged for her to meet her husband to be and that she is required to be at the introduction.

"I can get a man of my own. What is it so hard to understand Mama?" she had told her mother after her father left the room. She felt insulted.

"Sorry Rosetta, but we can't go against your father. Please get ready!" she said and left. Rosetta couldn't understand why they were deciding for her. Still, she didn't want to fight anymore. She had run out of options and so, she had to do as advised by her parents. After all, they said they meant well for her.

Rosetta had been matched before but she had not found anyone worth settling down with. She felt like they were just wasting her time. Finally, she got tired of the dating games and explored other options. And in her quest for true love, she went to a dating site and came up with an impressive profile. It caught many suitors' attention but she kept ignoring them. Until the day she came across Leonardo's profile. She could not help but notice the great photos he had shared.

"Ooh he looks so handsome!" Rosetta noticed. She zoomed in on the photo that was right before her eyes. She almost kissed her phone screen. She went through the many photos popping up slowly and very keenly. She could not help but wish she had someone just like him.

Rosetta was quick to notice that indeed, Leonardo had a great sense of fashion. Everything about him was trendy and classy. There were also other photos of him in a very big office and scrolling down the profile, she came across a company he managed. She promised herself she would visit the company one day and request to see him. But, she felt that it would make her look needy. Everything fell into place when he initiated a conversation through a chatroom. The messages kept coming and she gave in to his flow.

A few days later, they were both head over heels in love with each other. Their conversation was flowing perfectly and most of their likes and dislikes seemed the same. They had so many things in common. Their favorite meals, their dressing choices, and even their religious beliefs. They were both Catholics. The similarities were a good sign but also the unending compliments from Leonardo made him stand out from all her exes. He kept telling her that she was beautiful and he also loved seeing her in a dress.

And as usual, all was going well. She was getting ready for the visitors just as asked when more texts popped up. She had to sit down and reply. They were beautiful lines with the same magic touch as they always had. She didn't even hear her father walk in. She was carried away by the nice words coming from Leonardo. They continued to message each other.

"Please send me more photos of you in a dress. I just want to look at you today sweetheart. You are all I think about these days. You are the true definition of a beautiful woman," he texted. Rosetta read the text message and blushed.

"I'll send you one in a bit..." She was not sure which one of her photos to send. She went through her gallery and picked several. She then pressed the send button. Leonardo was so excited. Her father saw the message thread as he stood right behind her. He was disappointed in her. Still, he didn't talk to her so she continued to text since she didn't know he was there.

Ever since she was young, Rosetta always had self-esteem issues. She doubted her worth until that day Leonardo contacted her. He boosted her self-esteem in mysterious ways through compliments and shows of affection. He liked her and was ready to love her if given a chance.

To Rosetta, it was immense. She couldn't explain it but she could feel that there was something special about Leonardo. Other than the attractive face and muscles portrayed in his photos, he had quite an interesting personality.

He was also very different from all the other guys she had dated in the past. His sounded sincere and every word that he told her kept ringing in her mind. The way he said it, through messaging and calling. It unleashed a fire in her, so strong that she felt everything else come to a standstill. She was in a world of her own, a place where all things were perfect.

With time, her nights became warmer and calmer as she held her pillow thinking of him. An imaginary man who had the powers to keep her awake. It was a dream come true. If only she was sure about Leonardo but then, it was still too early to tell how serious he was. She imagined all the great times they would create together. She prayed and waited for a miracle to happen and bring him by her side before they took her to Eduardo.

Leonardo was a rare species. He made it known to her as soon as he started messaging her that he admired her. He expressed his innermost feelings and confessed to her how happy he would be if she loved him back. He wanted a chance to make her the most loved person in the world. And those words swept her off her feet. She was without a doubt the most important person in his life.

As their conversation continued, their bond grew stronger. He spoke about his life and even confided in her about many things. He mentioned that he didn't have parents that they were killed when he was young and he grew up in an orphanage. He was never lucky enough to get foster parents and his childhood was a struggle. The words created a bond between them. Rosetta felt sorry for him. She wanted to be a shoulder for him to lean on.

Well, Leonardo got what he wanted from her, total sympathy and attention.

Chapter 3

Within a few weeks of messaging, he was requesting for a face to face meeting. *How nice of him to ask,* Rosetta thought. Rosetta felt a deep connection between her and Leonardo.

It was coming true! Her prince charming was about to show up. Everyone who had thought she would never find true love was about to get a shock of a lifetime. They were all about to be put to shame more so her two younger sisters who had already gotten married and hurled all kinds of insults at her. It was time to prove to them that she was lovable. That someone as good-looking as Leonardo had noticed her. All that time, she had long forgotten about the expected visitors!

She stared at her phone in disbelief! Finally, a man was asking to meet her. She couldn't turn down such an offer. But just as she was about to type a yes to his request, someone tapped her shoulders. It was her father.

He looked at her full of disappointment. He had been there long enough and had seen the message thread. He wondered just how she could even be contemplating meeting a total stranger. Mr. Antonio felt heartbroken.

Three weeks ago, Mr. Antonio visited Mr. Lorenzo. They had planned on having a drink and discussing a few things regarding work. They owned a company together that dealt with auditing and basic accounting. They had been successful in the past few years and were very happy to see their success, but their discussion changed immediately after Eduardo came.

It was not like him to visit his parents unannounced. Worst of all, on a weekday. But what he wanted to discuss was urgent. It could not wait even a day. He had been going through a lot and even though, he was hurting, he had kept it from his family members for a long time. It was finally the best time to put everything out in the open.

There were wrangles in his marriage recently and he felt that they were taking a toll on him. His marriage was on the verge of breaking up. He wanted to file for divorce but he needed parental guidance, so he came to ask his parent's house for advice straight home from the office. It was a burning issue and he couldn't hold onto it anymore.

"It's okay son, you can talk to me in Antonio's presence. He is like family," suggested Lorenzo on seeing the discomfort written all over his son's face when he found Antonio seated across the table. But Antonio was ready to leave. He spoke.

"If it's a problem, and you need privacy it's okay, I can just leave," he said trying to ease the already rising tension among them but Lorenzo insisted that he stayed.

Eduardo explained everything that was going on. He didn't feel the spark anymore. He felt distant and his efforts to change or even address things were going unnoticed. Well, his parents never liked his wife. His mother claimed that she wasn't even Mexican and didn't even know how to cook Mexican dishes!

Every time they visited, her mother would spend the first sixty minutes complaining that her son was poorly fed. That he looked malnourished. She would rush to the kitchen and prepare Mexican dishes and then sit across admiring her son eating. She made Eduardo's wife, Elizabeth feel like she had failed.

Eduardo's parents didn't see the need to fight for the marriage. Their advice came as a shock to him. But on the other hand Antonio seemed to enjoy the advice they were offering. He brightened up when his friend, Lorenzo suggested that their son should look for a true Mexican. Someone with a strong background and more similarities than differences. And with that said, Mr. Antonio had a brilliant idea.

His idea was not the best but it was applauded by Lorenzo too. It would help in the company management generally as they had fifty-fifty ownership. And so they set up a meeting for the two young ones. The arrangement was treated like an emergency. They had to set the record straight and remove Eduardo's wife from the picture. After all, they had no child to tie Eduardo with child support. Eduardo was in for the idea.

Finally, the day came, and instead of Rosetta getting ready as requested, she had locked herself in her room going through Leonardo's profile and messaging him. Her father managed to twist the doorknob. He wanted to have a word with her as he had noticed that she wasn't taking the visit seriously. When he saw her sending photos to a stranger he could not hide his anger!

"Do you realize that we are doing this for you Rosetta?" he asked. His angry voice went through the walls and her mother came in. Maria observed her daughter keenly and chose not to speak. Rosetta sat there in silence. She felt that there was no need to explain anything to her parents. After all, they had decided to play matchmaker. They didn't even care about her feelings.

"Rosetta! Get up right now, go to the bathroom and freshen up. Apply something on your face. You need to look good for Eduardo to notice. You need to impress him." He meant it.

"Please go sweetheart. We all want the best for you baby girl," her mother said. Her father then left, leaving Maria behind. Rosetta turned and stared at her mother with resentment. She spoke...

"If you really wanted the best for me as you say, you should have allowed me to decide who I wanted to marry," but her words fell on deaf ears. Maria ignored her. She had no choice but clean up and join the rest of the family for dinner downstairs.

Leonardo continued texting. It was like he knew something was going on. Rosetta held her phone tightly, pressing it against her hand. A strong desire to meet Leonardo was starting to push her to extreme limits. Her father wanted her to get married to Eduardo while she wanted to try out her luck with Leonardo.

They waited for the guests to arrive as Maria kept smiling to herself. She was happy that finally, her first-born daughter was going to get a better match. Maria remembered the three exes her daughter had brought home back then. They looked so happy together and then boom, the relationships ended and the suitors disappeared. Maybe it was time to get involved in her dating life. They could help, maybe!

Finally, Lorenzo came accompanied by his wife and son. They were welcomed and food was served. They talked about a lot of things and at some point, the parents asked the children to give them some time. They wanted them to mingle, to learn about each other.

Rosetta stood up and took her phone with her. She had three unanswered texts from Leonardo. He wanted to know if she was ready for a meeting. She told him she was not ready to meet him yet but would love to in the near future. Rosetta wanted the matchmaking storm to calm down before they met. Leonardo didn't fight it. He totally understood that the right time would come and she would indeed come through.

When Rosetta and Eduardo came outside, each and every one took their own seats. They sat facing different sides. Rosetta was glued to her phone chatting with Leonardo as Eduardo closed his eyes in deep thoughts. He wanted to start a conversation but Rosetta wasn't interested. Still, he tried his luck to woo her.

"Do you believe in arranged marriages, Rosetta?" he asked. Rosetta feigned a smile.

"No, it's a total waste of time. I would rather live alone than have an arranged marriage," she said sarcastically.

"Then what are you doing here?" he wondered.

"The same as you, passing time." She was damn serious.

"Wait what, my marriage failed because I always choose bad girls., I want my parents to choose for me a life partner, and maybe it would work this time around." It sounded stupid to Rosetta.

"You think so?" she asked. It hit him so hard that he was stunned. He doubted himself and even questioned his sanity. Maybe Rosetta had a point, maybe it was too soon to move on.

Chapter 4

It was not easy for Eduardo, He thought he could easily dump Elizabeth and move on but his misery was evident even after the visit.

He sank down as he remembered the good times he had with his wife. They were great times indeed. To his surprise, he felt if life ever allowed him, again. He would gladly create more memories with her. He still missed her.

Like any other couple, they had had their own share of ups and downs. But it wasn't enough reason to walk away. His parents thought otherwise though after listening to his complaints.

The once strong love was affected by the many arguments that didn't end well. Initially, Eduardo thought it wise living apart for some time, terming it as a temporary separation or rather a break of some kind to put things between them in perfect order. But instead, Rosetta was brought in the limelight by his parents immediately after he moved to his parents' house. His move only worsened the storm between them. Things were never going to be the same again, not when his parents hated his woman. They advised him to try out someone else.

Later that day, after the guests left. Rosetta's family retired to bed earlier than usual. They had discussed a lot of things and each of them needed time to process. Rosetta's parents saw the idea as an amazing one. It would strengthen the bond they had with Lorenzo's family.

Strangely, Maria had a visitor in her sleep. It was Leonardo...and no, it was not just a dream. Leonardo was there in her bedroom!

"Hello Maria..." said Leonardo. He was sitting on one side of the bed comfortably counting the stars from where he was seated. The bedroom window was wide open as a soothing breeze filled the room. She pulled the duvet and covered her husband's legs. Then turned to Leonardo.

"You need to leave. My husband is going to wake up and you'll bring me more problems Leonardo," she said tensely.

"Not today dear. We made a deal and you are trying to ghost me! In case you forgot, I am not human so if you continue to ghost me, I will be a real ghost I assure you!" There was an uproar in the room as the windows crashed. Still, he was seated unmoved. Antonio woke up. Maria tried to push him away from the bed but he was too strong to move.

"Come on Maria, he can't see me unless I want him to," he said as he watched Antonio talk to his wife.

"Did you hear that?" he asked but Maria pretended to have been asleep.

"No, I heard nothing. Go back to sleep dear, there is nothing." she said and Antonio went back to sleep.

Maria remained awake. She was worried about her daughter. She had agreed to make a deal with a vampire since she didn't want to die. She knew Rosetta would be mad at her if she ever found out about her arrangement. But she had to as it was the only way they could leave the hospital alive. Leonardo spared them that day. After the incidence, he disappeared only to show up that night.

Maria lived her life believing that he had gone back to wherever he came from and would never come back to haunt them.

Indeed, Leonardo had been busy serving his master. He had broken so many rules in the vampire world and he was so scared of failing again. His only wish was to be with

Rosetta. It was something that he had worked for since the day he saw her at the hospital. His wish was about to be granted. But not under Maria's watch. She grinned as Leonardo disappeared into the dark.

***

Earlier That Day

"The only reason I agreed to this weird arrangement was because you were loyal, and always have been. You served me from your heart and I wanted to give you what you desired most in the world. I still can't believe you chose a woman over all the things you had power over. Why Leonardo?" the master questioned but Leonardo didn't want to talk about it.

He had been with Rosetta spiritually, watching her grow and protecting her so many times without her knowledge. But he was also to blame for the many mysterious things that kept happening in Rosetta's life, including the disappearance of her ex-boyfriends. He killed them all.

Leonardo had kept his promise. He said he would physically visit when Rosetta grew up. He came to remind Maria that she could easily lose her life for working together with Antonio yet she knew where Rosetta was destined to be, and with whom.

Leonardo was a patient man and had given her enough time to mature. He then approached her on a dating site. Even though he used someone else's photos, he was sure the young lady had developed feelings for him. He could tell by the kind of distraction she had the whole afternoon during Eduardo's visit. He was sure about one thing, he was going to win her with or without anyone's help. She was his.

***

Two Days Later

Antonio called Rosetta to join them during breakfast. She did and for the first time in a long time, she looked happy. She was dressed in a long red dress and greeted by everyone.

"Morning family," she said as she took her seat.

"Ooh, you look happy today...do you mind sharing with us?" Antonio said, but Maria interrupted him by asking if he needed more juice. She served them both and then sat down. She looked distant.

"Are you okay Mom?" asked Rosetta. Maria shook her hand. She lied she was fine but she wasn't, not after talking to Leonardo. Antonio turned to Rosetta.

"I hope you've thought about Eduardo, there is no turning back. A few months from now we'll be hosting your engagement party and a wedding will follow in a month's time," he said as he sipped the last drop of juice in his glass. Maria was shaken. She stammered and seemed out of place.

"We need to give them time to know each other well, to fall in love and connect without us forcing it on them. Even though they look so good together, we need to understand that they are grown-ups!" she said. Antonio could not believe what he had just heard. Since when did Maria start second-guessing him? Antonio didn't want to argue. He was actually late for work. He picked up his jacket and left. Maria knew that her daughter had questions about the whole turn around and so she left the table too. Rosetta continued to have breakfast alone.

Maria was going through a lot. She knew that she had to keep her word or lose her whole family. Rosetta was the only reason her whole family was still breathing. Maria made a promise to the devil himself after running out of options.

She never shared her story with anyone until recently when Leonardo showed up in her dream. She had thought that the vampire gave up but she was wrong. It appeared that he didn't and was back with a bang, very much willing to take back what was declared his many years ago.

Chapter 5

Thirty-five Years Ago

Maria went to deliver her first born daughter Rosetta. Even though she pretended to have forgotten, there were strange things that happened and reminded her that it was not all over. It made her scared, no matter how much she wanted to share. She was warned that the consequences would be far worse. For that reason, she kept it a secret even to her husband.

Maria remembered what transpired that day. She was feeling unwell and didn't want to disturb her husband who had been very busy with work. She decided to walk to the hospital which was not very far from her house. But along the way, her condition worsened and so she fell and lost consciousness. She lay by the roadside. People thought she was sleeping but she was fighting for her life. Suddenly someone saw her and decided to help.

Deep in the forest, sat the master, they called him father. It was a cemetery that had been forgotten decades ago. The vampires' family would all come together and discuss their progress. Each and every one of them had spoken apart from Leonardo. He had been pleading with his master to be allowed to mix with humans.

"I'm tired of your whining, I want you to go there and blend with the damn humans," his voice shook the ground. The trees went down breaking and there was a storm.

"You mean it Father?" he was excited.

"Yes but I want you to take your brother with you," he went on.

"Why? You know I don't like him, Father," he argued.

"That's exactly the reason I want him to go with you. Go hunt the humans and get the woman of your dreams. I will help you trace her. She will be born today....so hurry," he said and then walked back to the woods.

"Seriously Father you didn't give me the directions, a map or something," he said angrily.

"You are a vampire, find your way." He then disappeared.

Later that day, Leonardo found himself on the other side of the hospital. He laughed hysterically as cars passed, others hitting him while some crushed trying to escape from him. He was immortal. He couldn't even bleed. He had been given a chance to come back and mingle and finally get a chance to experience love.

It had been a long time since he had something to eat. He was thirsty for blood and the first place he spotted when he woke up was the hospital. He stood up and was about to go straight to the reception but along the way he spotted Maria. Immediately, he knew there was something in her. There was a strong connection. He wanted to help her and so he did.

"Humans are so heartless. How can motorists leave a pregnant woman on the street and drive to their destinations peacefully!" he bent down and picked her up. Finally, his master was impressed, he whispered to him.

"You did good son...now your wife is going to be born in this same hospital today. The same hospital that you are going to kill people. You will watch her and make sure she is delivered safely. If you make mistakes, I will get rid of you. You will never be heard or seen.." He made himself clear.

"Okay, I hear you Father! Can you stop with all the confusion you are causing me. You will destroy me if I fail you. FINE!!' he was running out of patience. His attention was carried away by the beautiful women around him.

"Hello beautiful, you look sweet," he was acting weird. He complimented every human being he met on his way. He still had Maria in his arms curled up like a baby. They both disappeared and only reappeared in the hospital in a flash. The receptionist was moody and ignored them but Leonardo's five minutes chat with her made her get back to her senses.

"I must admit you really are very beautiful but I am not human, so your beauty is the least of my concern. This is my wife. Will you help her get the medical attention she needs. I'm not requesting you, I'm ordering you!" he said grinning his teeth, he looked scary. Deep inside, he was salivating, he was hungry and thirsty and was so tempted to kill her. The temptations were so strong that holding back was a real struggle. Then the voice of his father came back.

"I told you. You can't change who you are no matter how hard you try. Look at the thirsty you!" he laughed at him. Leonardo was out of control. The receptionist thought he was a psycho. She pretended to be friendly to save the day and took in his patient. Maria was taken to the ward as Leonardo continued on his mission. He followed the receptionist closely. He couldn't take his eyes off her. He then started killing them one after the other starting with the receptionist!

"This feels good. I can't believe I waited that long." He didn't spare anyone on the corridors. He then made his way to the hospital wards. He fed on blood and every time he killed someone he would let out a crazy laugh until he got to Maria's ward. She had just given birth to a beautiful girl called Rosetta.

Leonardo bent down to her and smiled. Maria had no idea that the man standing before her had killed everyone in the hospital and had still saved her. Still he avoided her and didn't want her to recognize him. He wore a mask that made him look like one of the doctors. He even signed her discharge papers! Maria didn't know that the same man posing like a doctor was still, the same man who had carried her and brought her in to the hospital.

Well, there was one nurse who was still alive. The one who was taking care of Maria. They both didn't know that Leonardo had killed all of those people. They also didn't know that it was his nature to kill. He had done exactly what made him different from humans. His assignment had been to destroy as many humans as he could but Maria touched his heart. He felt sorry for her unborn child and that's why he helped her.

Looking at the little princess, there was no need to keep the nurse. She had done her work and was supposed to die like everyone else. The nurse noticed something off and wanted to inform the authorities but before she grabbed the phone, he got to her and killed her mercilessly. He laughed loudly as his body responded to the taste of human blood. All that while, his teeth remained out. His eyes turned red with every drop of blood he drank. The efforts by the police to arrest him were in vain.

The cops went on collecting bodies until they got to Maria. Nobody could believe how she had managed to survive there. When they informed her there was no one alive in the hospital, she panicked. She wanted to scream but she had no energy to do so. She wanted to go home and cool off. Suddenly a car drove to the parking lot. One of the men got out and said that he had come for his wife.

He came to the ward and assisted her with the baby. He wanted to take her home. She agreed even though she knew it was not her husband but she wanted to get out of that place. She got into the taxi and found another guy seated in the car. They were both middle-aged and were arguing about something.

"The old man only allowed you to come back here to do an assignment. Kill two hundred thousand people and go back! Simple!!" One said.

"And you think I don't know huh. I know but I want to make it right for one person. A deserving person. I will spare one. He said he would grant me my wish," said the other.

"You are not supposed to spare anyone! Humans have enjoyed this world for so long. We need to get rid of them and then have a place for us, just us! Don't you get it?" Maria was tense. She shook as the men spoke. She regretted agreeing to ride with them. It wasn't safe.

"Hey guys, I'm Maria." She spoke when she realized that they had forgotten about her. At first, she thought they were just thieves who wanted to steal and murder people but she was wrong. Their long teeth made her heart skip a bit. They were vampires!

Chapter 6

To her surprise, they didn't intend to kill her. They wanted to help her get home. Maria had many questions, she wondered why they were helping her. They didn't even know her. Her thoughts were suddenly interrupted by one of them.

"We know who you are, we are not going to hurt you...but we want a favor from..." he went on. Maria had to comply as she didn't want to lose her life. There was no point in arguing with vampires.

"Your beautiful girl, ooh she is such a cutie!" he touched her soft cheeks. Maria got back trying to prevent them from looking at her daughter. But one of them got hold of her hair and pulled her back.

"This is not a game. Do you think you are a special woman!? You aren't. I'll come for your daughter when she is fully grown. She will be my wife. And you will agree to it. That's the only way you and your handsome Antonio are going to live long enough to see tomorrow." His every word came out as a roar. She agreed but felt really sad to subject her daughter to all that.

"Before I forget, I will still look the same way I am right now. I don't grow old so don't worry, your daughter won't be marrying an older man...now get out of the car!" He made his point clear.

They dropped her home and Antonio was excited to see her. He hugged her and helped her walk to the house. He then made some tasty meals for Maria and they lived happily like they always did.

Life went back to the years when they were newly married. But even though the fling was strong between them, she could not share her story with her husband. She felt it was just a mere threat. Nothing would happen after all, how they would not even recognize her daughter when she'd be grown. Antonio was so busy with work that he didn't even notice anything wrong about his wife.

He went on with his daily activities and worked really hard to one day get to a company's director position. Having come from a middle-class family, it encouraged him to work harder to achieve his goals.

A lot of things kept happening without him noticing. However, it came to a point where he felt Maria needed help. He thought maybe it was the kids. He researched about postpartum depression and pointed at it as the main cause of his wife's predicaments. But it wasn't. Maria kept seeing images. She would see Leonardo on the streets and run away. It was not normal to behave in such a way. The neighbors claimed she was possessed by evil spirits.

She would scream loudly in her sleep and sometimes cry uncontrollably. He would try to talk to her but she insisted she was fine. He would then watch her sleep and go off to dreamland. He admired the chubby cheeks he had fallen in love with the very first time they met. Antonio remembered everything that transpired between them that day. The heavy rains, not forgetting the crazy traffic.

He vividly remembered how he had ignored traffic rules and resulted in being stopped by the police. The conversation went on for twenty minutes as the vehicles remained stuck on the road. Those that tried to find other ways or ever tried to go on the reverse were all apprehended. Antonio begged the cops to let him go as he had an early meeting with his then company's director. The cops didn't seem to buy any of what he was saying.

Maria's brother noticed the stare his sister was giving the young man and that made him even more furious. He pushed him harder. Like any other elder brother, he was overprotective of his little sister. But the said sister was not ready to quit. Instead, Maria felt so drawn into the young lad. Since it was raining, Maria sympathized with him and offered a nice treat that was readily available by then. She displayed enormous affection and moved near the accused man and generously spread out her umbrella. Maria covered Antonio, begged her brother to let him go. He was reluctant at first but finally bent the law and gave into his sister's persuasion. Maria and Antonio fell in love and the rest became history.

A journey of true love started to blossom at a higher knot. And just like that, the beautiful cheeks she fell in love with became the one feature that her babies took after genetically, huh, really beautiful genes they were.

Looking at him years later, he still gave her butterflies. Their spark was of a rare kind. It remained just as strong as it was when they first met. The truth was, there was nothing comparable to their affection. It took a lot more effort to get to such heights. Not just rubbing shoulders and sleeping effortlessly next to each other.

They planned their life together and walked the journey together for better, for worse.

* *

Thirty-five Years Later,

Leonardo was back in their lives and was not taking a no for an answer. After his appearance at night, Maria couldn't think straight. She tried her best to convince Antonio to let their daughter decide on who she wanted to live with but Antonio wasn't listening.

"Maybe we should encourage her more...the guy you told me about, the one she was messaging. Maybe they are a good match," she kept suggesting but Antonio had his own reasons. He understood that they had to have a bond for them to blend but still argued that it was not safe for her to meet a total stranger. But one thing Antonio didn't know, Leonardo wasn't a stranger!

"Our daughter needs someone we know better, a dedicated man and business minded. Look at Eduardo, he is that man," he argued.

"Well, maybe he is but remember, he left his wife just because they had a little misunderstanding. What if he does the same thing to our daughter?" she sounded worried.

"Hmm, would you rather she dated a stranger than someone we know, Maria. What has gotten into you?" he was confused.

Time went fast and within six months Eduardo proposed to her. He had fallen in love with her but she was thinking about someone else. She was thinking about Leonardo. The more Eduardo planned the engagement, the more Leonardo frequented Rosetta's bedroom. They spent nights together and in the morning she could not understand exactly what had happened. She was afraid to share the story and so she kept it to herself.

"You said you liked my name. Did you mean it?" She would ask in her dreams while clinging to his arms like a baby. She felt safer and always wanted the dreams to keep coming. They didn't stop! They kept happening and worsened with time when she started waking up to find her pants soaked. She knew that they were not dreams but in reality someone was having intimacy with her!

In the midst of confusion, she decided to lie awake one night to see her regular visitor. She made loud snores while faking sleep. Leonardo's shadow came in as usual through the window. He walked slowly and then started to kiss her lips. She wanted to stop him but his warm hands made her yearn for more. She tried to push Leonardo's mouth away, but she couldn't. He was too strong for her.

Leonardo was worried. He didn't want her to feel like he was forcing himself on her. He wanted her to desire him. To want him and to love him. He felt he had already messed up by becoming intimate with her without her consent.

He went on kissing her and seconds later she gave in to him. She kissed him back and held him close. Leonardo kissed her neck. She struggled to speak but she couldn't find the strength. She was carried away.

"Baby," she whispered. The word woke all his emotions and he held her tightly. He removed her pink nightdress and lay there naked waiting for her alpha male.

He was more than ready. He continued kissing her and within no time, he was on her breasts. They were soft and tender. He couldn't believe it when he saw them lying before him pointing at him. Her nipples were stiff as they reacted to the caresses Leonardo was giving her. He rubbed them slowly rhythmically. She was losing her breath.

Chapter 7

He loved seeing her like this.

She had desired his touch for so long. He then licked her body from head to toe and stopped at the breast once again. It had become his favorite spot. He bite the nipples a little, and she moved her body upward. Their bodies touched as his dick became erect.

She could feel his strength, he was so strong and firm. She was also dripping wet. Her vagina wanted him more and more. She opened her legs wide open and got ready for him. Instead, he asked her to come on top and ride.

Seconds later she was in control. Leonardo was moaning so loudly. His eyes turned red and scary. He couldn't control the monster in him. He held her with all his strength and turned her over. He was on top of her and pumping her. His cock was huge and the more they fucked the more it hit the side of the vagina. She was scared but she loved his energy.

Fifteen minutes later, he was still pumping. His face suddenly started to change color. His eyes became blood-like. He increased his breathing. His hands began shaking. He wasn't cumming. Instead, his vampire self came back. He was not Leonardo. His face was bleeding and so was Rosetta's pussy. She was asking him to stop but he couldn't stop. He pumped her harder and stronger that he ended up hurting her.

When he got back to his senses, he apologized and then licked her vagina. He needed to get the blood off her. He swallowed it. Rosetta looked at him like a devil. She was scared but she could not scream.

"Are you honestly really doing that? That's blood...you bruised me. I can't even walk!" she complained.

"Sorry baby, I'll bring a lubricant tomorrow sweetheart," he said confidently but she wasn't content. She wanted answers and better still, a stop to the madness that was going on at night.

"This is not happening again. The two months you've been visiting are enough. You need to stop!" she said angrily. Instead, Leonardo was focusing on her lips in the moonlight. The windows were still opened since it was the only way he would get in the room. They could see the outside and the moon seemed to light the bedroom. It was the best feature.

"Do you really think it's easy to stop?" he asked. Rosetta answered him very fast. She said it was but Leonardo moved closer to her lips.

"I know it's not, not with the intimacy we have had over the two months. Whenever I come near you, even in a dream, you always tremble...and you think that that is easy...ha-ha, don't lie to me sweetheart!" He went on as he kissed her lips. She trembled again but stood her ground. Whatever it was, it had to stop.

"Maybe, that's what you feel. But I have come to realize that my father knows what is good for me. So I'm going to....." she was interrupted by another kiss.

"You didn't say that earlier today. You said you couldn't wait to see me!" he said. He was thinking of revealing himself to her.

"Wait, who are you?" she was confused.

"I'm your guardian angel," he said but to her it was just another lie.

"Ha ha that's what everyone says. You always sneak into my room and make love to me. I've never seen your face. Are you a ghost or something?" she asked, confused.

"I'm the guy you message.. I'm your secret admirer," he clarified things but Rosetta couldn't believe it.

"Are you some kind of a ghost because one thing I know you aren't human. I mean who fucks like that!" she laughed sarcastically and it made the pain come back. She pulled her legs back together.

"I wanted you not to attend the engagement party tomorrow. I don't want you to go," he begged her.

"Sorry but I have to. I'm tired of dating and this is the right guy for me," she had made up her mind.

"But you said you wanted us to try this. You said you loved my energy last night!" he wanted her to reconsider.

"Look, whatever I have been telling you during intimacy is pure madness. You've been sneaking in and out! And look the man on the app isn't you. He is tall and has short hair. He also doesn't have a bushy beard. You do. It's not you I know that," she said, running out of patience.

"Maybe, I used the photos because I didn't want you to get scared of me. I was only trying to impress you," he was on his knees, and suddenly someone touched the doorknob. He had to go. He kissed her and disappeared into the moonlight. He was invisible.

Her mother stood at the door wondering if indeed she was talking in her dreams like she had been doing.

"Rosetta! Rosetta!" she called but she pretended to be asleep. She wasn't and could hear her just fine but she wasn't interested in long lectures. Her mother then pulled the sheets and covered her.

"She must be talking again! This girl is something else!" she said as she walked out of the room.

Rosetta spent the rest of the night awake. She couldn't help but think of Leonardo. He was great and told her exactly what she wanted to hear. She loved his energy in bed and wished to have him lie next to her all the days of her but it was not easy considering the next day.

Morning came, she was moody and so was her mom.

"Hey baby, I miss you and I can't wait to see you," he said.

"Hmm," she was silent. Since the previous night, she was having doubts. There was a lot at stake. She had just told Eduardo she loved him. She hated breaking his heart.

Her father had been at the forefront waiting for Eduardo to visit. He had promised to engage Rosetta that day. The few months were enough for courtship. There was no need to waste more time. The wedding plans were also in progress, the only remaining thing was a date which was for Rosetta to decide.

"You love me too I know and this is going to work, trust me," he assured her but she was thinking about Leonardo.

Eduardo had them picked up and taken to the venue. She was aware that Eduardo wanted to get engaged and with her father on her case, there was no turning back. She didn't want to hurt her father. They were all excited to be there. To witness their daughter getting engaged. People had drinks as they danced to soothing Mexican music. But Maria kept hearing voices in her head.

"So you've decided to give away your daughter to someone who doesn't even love her. Isn't that selfishness?!?" Leonardo asked..

"Her father has refused to listen to me. I have no other option," Maria said, defending herself.

"So you're backing out. How foolish. I only spared you because of your daughter. You and your husband are breathing because you had to raise her. She can't get engaged to anyone else otherwise, the lucky suitor is going to die like the others," the voices went on. She left the party and went to catch some air.

"And now that you have failed to honor our deal, I'm going to get her myself. I will stop the engagement!" Maria was going crazy. Suddenly it was all quiet. The clouds gathered as people waited for Rosetta to answer.

Just as promised, Leonardo took the ring that Eduardo had bought for her and posed the question himself.

"Rosetta Antonio, will you marry me and make me the happiest man in the world sweetheart?"

"Yes!! Yes!!I will marry you!" she was so happy to finally get a man of her dreams!

THE END

www.ingramcontent.com/pod-product-compliance
Lightning Source LLC
Chambersburg PA
CBHW020135180726

47992CB00023B/3182